This book belongs To

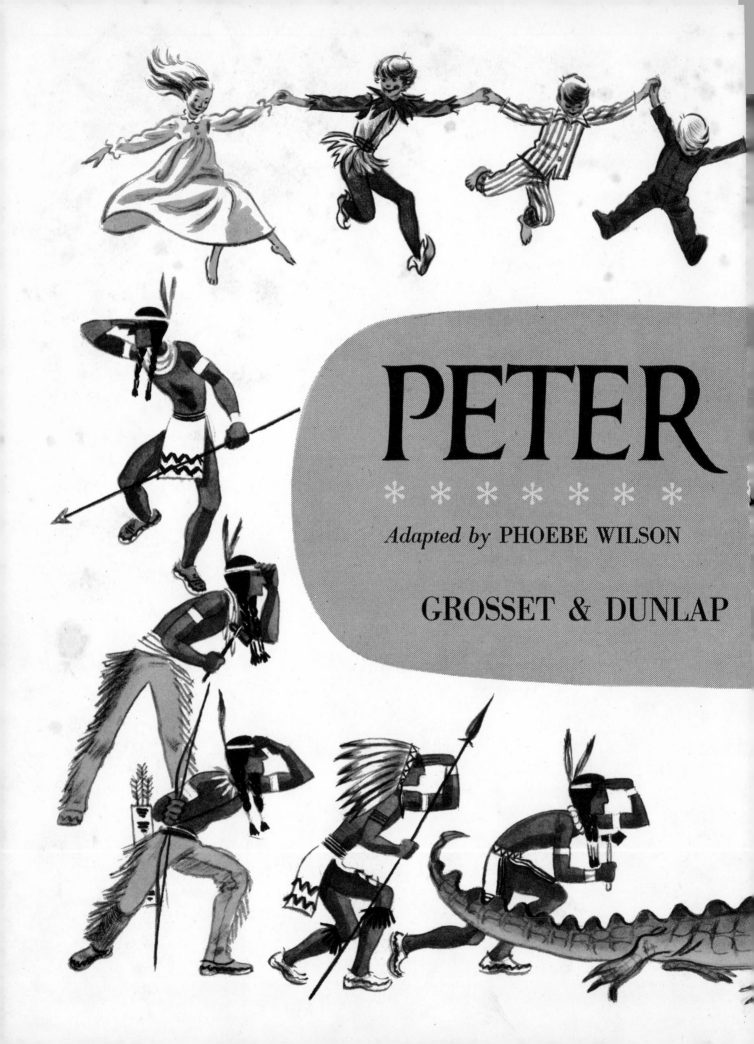

PETER

* * * * * *

Adapted by PHOEBE WILSON

GROSSET & DUNLAP

PAN

Illustrated by RUTH WOOD

✳ ✳ ✳ ✳ ✳ ✳ ✳

PUBLISHERS · NEW YORK

ISBN: 0-448-02137-4 (Trade Edition)
ISBN: 0-448-03681-9 (Library Edition)

© by Grosset & Dunlap, Inc., 1956, 1963

Published 1911 under the title of PETER AND WENDY.
Published 1921 under the title of PETER PAN AND WENDY.

1971 PRINTING

WENDY and John and Michael would never have left home if Nana had not been tied up outdoors for the evening. Nana was the children's nurse and she was not usually tied up—even though she was a huge Newfoundland dog. Usually she slept in a kennel in their room to see that they didn't get into any mischief during the night.

But Mr. and Mrs. Darling—Wendy and John and Michael's mother and father—had never quite agreed on the advantages of having a dog for a nurse. Mrs. Darling pointed out how carefully Nana walked the children to school in the morning, carrying an umbrella in her mouth in case of rain. Only Nana could persuade the children to take their medicine at night. But Mr. Darling scowled and said that Nana acted as though the children were her puppies. Nevertheless, up until now, Mr. Darling had never had an excuse for punishing the dog.

It was early evening and Nana was getting the children ready for bed. Mrs. Darling sat by the fire in the bedroom. Then Mr. Darling came in, all dressed for the party. Rushing forward to greet him, Nana jumped up and put her paws on his shoulders.

"Down, Nana!" he ordered. He brushed his coat sleeves rapidly. "Now see what that dog has done! It's gotten hairs all over my new suit." He was so annoyed at Nana that he decided to chain her outdoors for the night. "Dogs don't belong in a house, anyway," he said as he put on her collar around her neck.

"No, no, no," cried Wendy and John and Michael, who came in just as their father started to lead Nana away.

Nana wagged her tail as hard as she could, but Mr. Darling would not change his mind. "Out in the yard with you," he said briskly. "That's the place for dogs!"

Mrs. Darling tucked the children into bed and told them a story. Then she and Mr. Darling turned out the lights and left for their party.

Wendy and John and Michael fell asleep at once, so they did not see the soft light that suddenly whirled into their room. It glowed on the mantel, flashed to the bureau, flew from chair to chair. When it was still, one could see that it was a tiny, lovely fairy. A moment later a boy dressed in green leaves and wearing a green cap with a sweeping feather glided through the open window of the bedroom.

Silently he flew over each bed to make sure the children were asleep. Then he called softly, "Tink! Tinker Bell! Have you found my shadow?"

Tinker Bell answered Peter in fairy language, which sounded exactly like tinkling little golden bells. She said his shadow was in the bottom of the bureau. Peter leaped to the bureau and, sure enough, there was his thin gray shadow. He shut the drawer without noticing that Tinker Bell had disappeared, and began to fasten his shadow to his feet.

But try as he would, he couldn't get it to stick. Neither soap nor water nor fairy dust would do. He sat down on the floor and began to cry.

His sobs woke Wendy, and she sat up in bed to see who it was.

"Hello, boy," she said politely. "Why are you crying?"

Peter jumped to his feet and bowed. "What's your name?" he asked.

"Wendy Moira Angela Darling," she replied. "What is yours?"

"I am Peter Pan," he said grandly. "I'm from Neverland."

"Goodness!" exclaimed Wendy. "Where's that?"

"Second turning to the right, and then straight on till morning."

"What a funny address! Is that where you get your letters?"

"Don't get letters," he said scornfully.

"Well, surely your mother does."

"Don't have a mother," he said even more scornfully.

"Oh, Peter — no wonder you were crying!"

"I wasn't crying about mothers," he protested. "I was crying because I can't get my shadow to stick on."

"I'll sew it on for you," Wendy offered, jumping out of bed and getting a needle and thread. She knelt on the floor and quickly stitched the shadow to Peter's heels. The needle hurt a bit, but Peter did not cry out. And when the shadow was on, he turned handsprings. He forgot that Wendy had sewn the shadow on. He thought he had done it himself.

"How clever I am!" he crowed gleefully. "Cock-a-doodle-doo!"

Wendy was shocked. "You conceited boy!" she exclaimed. "I suppose I did nothing!"

"You did a little," said Peter carelessly. But then he added quickly, "Wendy, don't be angry. You're really worth twenty boys."

"Do you really think so, Peter?" Wendy asked, smiling. "How nice of you to say that! Let me give you a kiss for that."

Peter did not know what she meant by a kiss. But he saw the pretty silver thimble on Wendy's finger and thought she must mean that. He put out his hand for it. Wendy was surprised, but she was too kind to tell Peter he was mistaken. So she handed him the thimble.

Then Peter said, "Now let me give you a kiss." And he presented her with an acorn he had brought all the way from Neverland.

"Thank you, Peter," said Wendy, smiling. She put it carefully in the pocket of her nightgown. "Now, tell me all about Neverland."

Peter sat cross-legged on the bed and told her about his life in Neverland with the Lost Boys. He was their Captain, he said, and they all lived together in an underground home in the woods. They were friends with a nearby tribe of Indians, but they fought pirates who lived on a ship in the lagoon.

"Haven't you ever had a mother?" asked Wendy pityingly.

"Once I did," he answered. "When I was very little, I heard her talking to my father about what I would be when I grew up. But I didn't ever want to grow up," he exclaimed. "I wanted always to be a boy and have fun. So I ran away and lived with the fairies."

"Oh, Peter! How exciting!" said Wendy. "Tell me about the fairies."

"Well, there's one here now. I wonder where she's hidden herself." Suddenly he began to laugh. "Wendy" he whispered gleefully, "I do believe I shut her up in the drawer!"

He ran across the room and pulled open the bottom bureau drawer. Out flew poor Tinker Bell, and she was tinkling with fury.

The lovely golden fairy kept flitting around the room, tinkling in her anger at Wendy, whom she did not like. Peter turned his back on her and went back to answering Wendy's questions.

"But why do you come here?" Wendy asked.

"To hear the stories your mother tells you," he answered. "Since none of us has any mother, we don't know any stories. Oh, Wendy," he said suddenly, "why don't you come to Neverland to live with me and the Lost Boys and be our mother and tell us stories?"

"But how can I go with you?" Wendy protested. "I can't fly."

"I'll teach you. We'll jump on the wind's back and away we'll go."

"What about John and Michael?" she asked. "May they come, too?"

"Of course," said Peter. "They can be Lost Boys."

Wendy ran to John and Michael and shook them. "Peter Pan has come to take us to Neverland," she cried. "He is going to teach us to fly."

Both boys were awake and out of bed in a twinkling.

"Oh, boy!" shouted John. "Can you really fly, Peter?"

For an answer, Peter flew around the room. It looked so easy that the children tried jumping off the bed and flapping their arms, but they just fell down. Then Peter blew a puff of fairy dust on each of them. "Now," he said, "wriggle your shoulders like this and let go."

Michael, the youngest, was first. "I flew!" he screamed while still in mid-air. A moment later Wendy and John were flying round and round the room, too. "Look at me! Look at me!" they shouted.

15

Peter stood on the windowsill with Tinker Bell hovering at his shoulder. "Are you all ready to go?" he cried.

"Yes!" they shouted together.

And out of the window they flew, with Peter crowing triumphantly and Tinker Bell lighting the way ahead. They flew through the sleeping city and out over the ocean. They flew that night and all the next day. It seemed as though they were going to fly forever when Peter pointed and shouted, "There's Neverland! There!" And there it was, a round tree-covered island with a stream running through it. In a far lagoon a pirate ship was riding at anchor.

John asked who was the Captain of the pirate ship.

"James Hook," answered Peter, and his face became very stern. "He was Blackbeard's bo'sun — the worst pirate of them all. But I once cut off a bit of his right hand. Now he has a hook there, and he claws with it."

At this awful picture everyone shivered and moved closer together in the gloomy twilight air. For it had been getting steadily darker since they had sighted the island. Suddenly Tinker Bell flew to Peter and whispered in his ear.

"Tink tells me," said Peter, "that the pirates spotted us before it got dark, and they are waiting for us with Long Tom, their big gun. I think we had better fly in separately. Tink, you lead Wendy," he commanded, "and I will take Michael and John."

And so they parted in the darkness. Tinker Bell flew ahead of Wendy, muttering angrily. But to Wendy the tinkle of her voice sounded lovely. She didn't realize that the fairy would like to lead her to her doom.

17

CAPTAIN HOOK

Below on the island, grim Captain Hook was making one of his many searches for the home of Peter Pan and the Lost Boys. As he stalked through the woods with his bo'sun Smee, he sang a menacing pirate song:

"Avast, belay, when I appear,
By fear they're overtook.
Nought's left upon your bones when you
Have shaken claws with Hook."

The two men came to a clearing in the woods and sat down to rest on a large mushroom. Hook was tall and swarthy with coal-black hair that curled to his shoulders. As he spoke, he smoothed his drooping mustache with his dreadful claw.

"Most of all," he said heatedly, "I want their captain, Peter Pan, who cut off my hand. I've waited long to shake his hand with this." And he shook his shining claw threateningly.

"And yet," said Smee, "I have often heard you say the hook was worth a dozen hands, for combing hair and the like."

"Aye, that's true," said Hook. He frowned darkly. "What I hate Pan for is that he flung my hand to a crocodile. And that crocodile liked my hand so much, Smee, that it has followed me from sea to sea and from land to land, licking its lips for the rest of me."

"In a way," said Smee, "it's a sort of compliment."

"I want no such compliments," Hook barked crossly. "I want Peter Pan, who first gave the brute its taste for me. That crocodile would have had me before this, but by a lucky chance it swallowed a clock which ticks inside it. And so, before it can reach me, I hear the tick and bolt." He laughed hollowly.

"But some day the clock will run down and then . . ." Smee did not finish.

"Aye," said Hook, "that's the fear that haunts me."

Suddenly Hook leaped from his seat. "This mushroom is burning hot," he exclaimed.

He and Smee examined the mushroom, which was larger than the ordinary kind. When they tried to pull it up, it came away at once in their

hands. Smoke poured out of a hole in the ground where it had been. The pirates looked at one another.

"A chimney!" they muttered. Then they heard voices.

"The Lost Boys!" whispered Hook triumphantly. "Peter Pan's boys! Now I've got them! This is their home." But before he could think of a way to trap them, he heard another sound, faint at first but steadily louder.

Tick, tock, tick tock!

Hook shuddered. "The crocodile!" he gasped. And he bounded away through the woods, followed by his bo'sun. It was indeed the crocodile, which slithered through the clearing on its way after Hook.

WENDY ARRIVES

On the trail of the crocodile came one of the Lost Boys of Neverland, Nibs, who had been out to see if there was any sign of Peter's return. He ran panting to one of the tall trees surrounding the clearing and called down it.

"Come up quickly," he cried. "A great white bird is flying this way."

"What kind of a bird is it?" called the boys from below.

"I don't know," Nibs said, "but it looks weary, and as it flies, it moans, 'Poor Wendy.' Do come and see."

A minute later several boys appeared. First came the serious Tootles, and then Slightly, whistling as usual. He was followed by mischievous

Curly. And last of all came the Twins. Dressed alike in bearskin suits, they were so furry and round that they rolled as they tumbled out of their home.

Wendy was now almost overhead, and they could hear her mournful cry. Ever since leaving Peter, Tinker Bell had pinched and taunted Wendy who was too tired from the long flight to resist. But by now the jealous fairy had flown away, not wishing the boys to know how cruel she had been. Suddenly Wendy could fly no longer. And as the Lost Boys watched and wondered at the strange white bird, she fluttered to the ground.

There she lay, very still in her white nightgown. The boys crowded around her. Slightly was the first to speak. "This is no bird," he said. "I think it must be a lady."

"A lady?" asked Tootles, who didn't remember ever seeing one before.

"A lady to take care of us," said Nibs.

"Now I see," Curly said, "Peter must have been bringing her to us."

"And he must have lost her," said the Twins, "and now she is dead."

"Cock-a-doodle-doo-oo!" Peter's crow echoed through the forest. The next moment he dropped to the ground in front of the boys.

"Boys!" he cried. "I have wonderful news. I have a mother for you all at last. Have you seen her? She flew this way."

"Peter," Tootles said sadly, "we have seen her. We think she is dead." And the boys all stood back to let Peter see. But before he could say a word, Wendy moved her arm.

"She lives! She lives!" the boys all cried.

"Of course," said Peter, as he knelt beside her. "She has only fainted."

"Shall we take her down to the cave?" asked Tootles.

"No," answered Peter, "we cannot get her down a tree like this. We will build a little house around her up here. Quick, boys," he ordered, "get to work and build a house."

Immediately the boys scurried to get wood and moss to build a house. When John and Michael appeared out of the woods, Peter put them to work, too. In no time at all, Wendy was hidden inside a little wooden house with a soft, mossy roof.

The next day the boys hollowed out trees for Wendy and John and Michael, so each had one to take him to the great cave under the ground which was their home. Soon all three were as happy as though they had never lived in any other home.

In one wall of the cave there was a hole, no bigger than a birdcage. This was Tinker Bell's private room. It was elegantly furnished and glowed with Tink's lovely light.

DANGER IN THE LAGOON

On long summer days the boys and Wendy swam and splashed in the blue waters of the lagoon. Wendy, like a proper mother, made them stretch out after lunch for a nap on a large rock in the middle of the lagoon. One day while the boys were dozing and Wendy sat darning their socks, a change came over the lagoon. The water shivered, and the sun went away. It began to get dark and there was a chill in the air—the chill of danger. In the distance there was the sound of muffled oars.

Suddenly Peter awoke and leaped to his feet. He crowed his warning crow. "Pirates!" he cried. And then he ordered, "Dive!"

Splash! Instantly into the water went ten pairs of legs. The boys circled silently out around the rock, while Peter and Wendy stayed on it, out of sight.

A boat drew near the deserted rock. It was the pirate dinghy, and in it were three people—Smee, a fellow pirate called Starkey, and the Indian princess, Tiger Lily. That very afternoon Captain Hook had caught her trying to board his ship with a knife in her mouth. He had ordered Smee and Starkey to take her to this lonely rock and leave her there to drown when the waters rose.

"Luff, you lubber," cried Smee. "Here's the rock. Now, then, put down the lantern and help me toss the Indian out." In a moment they had hoisted the beautiful Indian onto the rock.

Nearby, Wendy was crying silently for she had never seen or heard of anything so wicked. Peter was determined to save Tiger Lily. It might have been easier to wait until the pirates had left, but he never chose the easy way when he saw adventure ahead. He could imitate all kinds of voices, and now he spoke in the gruff, deep tone of Captain Hook.

"Ahoy, there, you lubbers!" he called. "Set the Indian free. Cut her bonds and let her go."

"Let her go?" gasped the pirates. "But, Captain . . ."

"At once!" cried Peter. "Do ye hear?"

"Better do what the Captain orders," said Starkey nervously.

"Aye, aye," Smee answered, and he cut Tiger Lily's cords. At once she slid off the rock and disappeared into the water.

But then—"Boat ahoy!" rang over the dark lagoon in Hook's voice. And this time it was not Peter who had spoken. Captain Hook himself was also in the water.

Smee and Starkey heard him swimming to the boat, and they raised their lantern to guide him. In the flickering light Wendy saw his hook grip the boat's side, and she saw his dark and evil face as he climbed over.

Captain Hook sat down in the boat without a word. He gloomily rested his head on his hook.

At last he spoke. "The game's up, men. Those boys have found a mother!"

"A mother!" exclaimed Smee and Starkey together.

"Aye," said the wicked Captain, tossing his black curls. "And with a mother to help him, I shall never catch Peter Pan."

"Captain," suggested Smee, "why couldn't we kidnap the boys' mother and make her our own mother?"

The Captain smiled an evil smile. "A princely scheme!" he cried. "We can seize them all and carry them to the ship. We will make the boys walk the plank, and Wendy shall be our mother. What say you, my bullies?"

"There is my hand on it," both men said.

"And there is my hook."

Suddenly Hook remembered Tiger Lily. "Where is the Indian?"

"She's all right, Captain," Smee answered complacently. "We let her go."

"Let her go?" cried Hook.

" 'Twas your own orders," the bo'sun faltered.

"You called out to us to let her go," added Starkey.

"Brimstone and gall!" thundered Hook. "I gave no such order. But I can guess what clever fiend had a hand in this." He roared. "Peter Pan!"

Peter could not restrain his pride. "Yes," he called across the water. "It was I, Peter Pan."

"Now we have him," Hook shouted. "Into the water, men. Take him dead or alive."

Over the dark waters came Peter's gay voice. "Are you ready, boys?"

"Aye, aye," they answered.

"Then after the pirates. Quick. Cock-a-doodle-doo!"

The fight was short and sharp. Here and there a head bobbed in the water, and a flash of steel was followed by a cry or a whoop. But no one dared go near Captain Hook with his terrible claw.

Finally Hook climbed up on the rock to breathe. At the same time Peter went up on the opposite side. Neither knew the other was coming. When they arrived at the top, they raised their heads. And so they met.

Quick as a thought Peter snatched a knife from Hook's belt. But quicker even than he was the iron hand. Twice it clawed him. Before Peter could strike back, a new sound came softly across the lagoon.

Tick, tock, tick, tock!

Hook quivered and turned pale. "The crocodile," he muttered. Without another look at Peter, he was off the rock and swimming for the dinghy, with his two men close behind him.

When the other boys saw the pirates swimming away, they knew the fight was over. They looked around for Peter and Wendy, but there was no sign of them in the dark lagoon.

"They must have flown home," Tootles said. "We had better follow."

In the dark no one had noticed the two small figures lying on the rock. Wendy had fainted and Peter was too weak to call after the boys. Finally Wendy stirred, and Peter spoke to her.

"We are on the rock, Wendy, but there is less and less room on it. The tide is rising and soon the rock will be covered."

"Oh, Peter, what shall we do?" cried Wendy. "Can't we fly?"

"No," said Peter sadly. "Hook wounded me. I can neither fly nor swim."

"And I am too tired to fly alone," moaned Wendy.

Just then something brushed against Peter's cheek. It was the tail of a kite Michael had let loose that morning. With a feeble crow, Peter jumped up and grabbed it. He began to tie its tail around Wendy.

"Now," he said, "it can carry you home."

"Why not both of us?" asked Wendy.

"It can't lift two," said Peter bravely. "Michael and Curly tried."

Before Wendy could say another word, he pushed her from the rock and she was lifted into the air.

The rock seemed very small now. Soon it would be covered. Peter stood, watching the waters rise. Then he noticed an odd thing floating toward him. It looked like a piece of paper. Soon it came so close that he could see it. It was the Never Bird, floating on her nest.

Peter was about to turn away when she called to him.

"Get into the nest," she croaked, "and then you can drift ashore."

She brought the nest close to the rock and flew up over Peter's head. Crowing happily, Peter got into the nest and began to paddle with his hands. The bird flew along ahead of him. When he got to the shore he jumped onto the sand and crowed his thanks. Then he skipped off through the forest to join Wendy and the boys.

THE PIRATES ATTACK

After Peter's rescue of Tiger Lily, the Indians were so grateful that they came every night to guard the cave against pirate attack.

One evening after supper, Wendy gave the boys each a tablespoonful of their make-believe medicine and tucked them into bed before their story. On this evening she told the only story Peter hated — the story of Mr. and Mrs. Darling and their three children, Wendy, John and Michael. It always ended with the children returning home. Peter hated it because he was afraid, when she told it, that some day Wendy would want to leave Neverland and go home.

When she got to the end this night, Michael leaned out of his basket and said, "Wendy, aren't you really our mother?"

"No," she answered, "I'm only a make-believe one."

"Of course, she isn't," said John. "But," he added, "are you really sure, Wendy, that Mother and Father will be waiting for us?"

"Yes, yes, I think so," said Wendy.

"I think we should make sure," said Michael.

"Yes, Wendy, let's go home before it's too late," said John.

"All right," she said a little sadly. "We will go home at once." She turned to Peter. "Will you arrange it, Peter?"

Peter was very hurt at her wishing to leave so suddenly. But he was too proud to show it. So he just said, "Of course," and started to plan their trip. He strode up and down the room saying, "I will ask the Indians to guide you through the woods, and Tinker Bell will take you across the sea."

"Thank you, Peter," said Wendy, wishing she didn't have to leave him and the Lost Boys behind. Suddenly she clapped her hands and said, "Why don't you all come with me? My mother and father will adopt you."

The boys, who had been feeling very sad at the thought of her leaving, jumped out of bed and rushed to get their things. But Peter didn't move.

"You are coming, too, aren't you, Peter?" asked Wendy, alarmed.

"No, Wendy," he said. "I don't want to have a mother and grow up." And to show her that he didn't care about her leaving, he skipped up and down the room, playing gaily on his pipes. Wendy followed him, trying to coax him to come. But he only kept on playing.

Then the boys all gathered round to say good-by. Each boy carried a stick over his shoulder and on each stick was a bundle tied in a bandanna. Peter shook hands with them and with Wendy, and he said he hoped they would all enjoy family life.

Wendy kissed him gently on the forehead and said, "Good-by, Peter, and remember to take your medicine."

"I will," said Peter. And then he called to Tinker Bell. "Are you ready?"

"Aye, aye," she tinkled.

Suddenly the peaceful night was shattered. Steel rang against steel. There were bloodcurdling shrieks and cries. The pirates had attacked the Indians! No one spoke. Everyone looked to Peter for protection. Peter seized his sword and started to mount his tree. Then the noise of the struggle ended as quickly as it had begun. But—which side had won?

Above ground the pirates, listening at the hollow trees, heard Peter say, "If the Indians have won, they will sound the tomtom. It is their sign of victory."

At these words, Hook turned with an evil smile and signaled to Smee to beat the tomtom. Twice the victorious drum throbbed through the forest.

The children heard it and they cheered. Once more they said good-by to Peter and began to come up out of their trees. At each tree a pirate waited. Before they could cry out, the children were bound and gagged and carried off to the pirate ship. Only Tinker Bell escaped. She flew along behind the pirates and their captives to see what would happen.

Captain Hook remained behind to take care of Peter Pan himself. He dropped his black plumed hat on the grass and stepped into the biggest tree. Holding his knife in his teeth, he slid silently into the darkness.

Down at the bottom, he peered over the half-door. There on the bed, out of his reach, lay Peter, fast asleep.

Hook took a stealthy step to open the door. But he found that he did not have enough room to bend down to reach the latch. Was his enemy to escape him after all?

Then he saw Peter's medicine in a glass on a shelf within easy reach. Out of his pocket Hook took a small bottle of poison and poured five drops of it into Peter's glass. Gloating, he wormed his way back up the tree. He put on his hat and wrapped his coat around him. And, muttering to himself, he sped off toward his ship.

PETER TO THE RESCUE

Peter slept on. In his dreams he felt a soft, light tapping on his cheek. He awoke to see Tink flying above him, her dress stained with mud. Before he could say a word, she poured out the story of the capture of Wendy and the boys.

Peter got angrier and angrier as he listened. "I'll rescue her!" he cried, leaping out of bed. Then he thought of something he could do to please her. He could take his medicine. And he raised the glass to drink.

But Tinker Bell knew that the evil Hook had poisoned it. With a lightning movement, she got between Peter's lips and the glass and drank the medicine to the last drop.

"How dare you drink my medicine?" asked Peter furiously.

But she did not answer. Already she was reeling in the air.

"What is the matter with you!" cried Peter, suddenly afraid.

"Hook poisoned the medicine, Peter," she told him softly, "and now I am going to die."

She fluttered weakly to her room and lay down on the bed. Her light was dimming fast. Peter knew that if it went out she would be dead.

He knelt beside her. "What can I do to help you?" he asked.

In a faint voice she answered, "I think I could get well if I knew that children believed in fairies."

Peter stood up and spoke to all children who might be dreaming of Neverland.

"Do you believe in fairies?" he cried. "If you believe," he shouted again to sleeping children everywhere, "clap your hands, so Tink can hear. Don't let her die."

From all over the world the sound of millions of children clapping echoed back to Neverland.

Tinker Bell was saved. First, her voice grew stronger. Then she popped out of bed. And soon she was flashing through the room, merry as ever.

"And now to rescue Wendy," said Peter.

The moon was riding high when he set out with his weapons. The forest was very still. He crept silently along the path to the ship. Now he crawled forward like a snake. Now he raced across a space lit by the moon. And as he went, he vowed, "Hook or me this time."

On the way he passed the crocodile. Only after it had disappeared among the trees did he realize that it had not disturbed the stillness of the woods. It no longer ticked. The clock had run down and stopped at last!

At once Peter decided that he would tick so that wild beasts would think he was the crocodile and let him pass. He ticked superbly. So superbly that the crocodile, who heard the sound, followed him.

When Peter reached the shore, he plunged into the water and headed for the ship, still ticking. Suddenly, as he swam, he realized how he might use the ticking to trick Captain Hook.

At this moment, the Lost Boys and John and Michael were being lined up on deck. They were about to walk the plank. Poor Wendy was tied to the mast. And Captain Hook was smiling at his cleverness in ridding himself of all his enemies so swiftly.

Then he heard it—tick, tock, tick, tock! The pirates froze. Hook forgot about the boys and remembered only the dreaded crocodile. He fell to his knees and crawled along the deck as far from the sound as he could go.

"Hide me," he cried hoarsely. His pirates gathered around him and fearfully turned their backs on the terrible thing that seemed to be coming over the side. Only the boys and Wendy saw that it was Peter. He signaled them to say nothing and tiptoed into the ship's cabin and shut the door. The ticking stopped.

After a moment, Smee turned around and said, "It's gone, Captain. All's still again."

Hook listened carefully. There was not a sound. He stood up, smiling grimly, and walked over to the boys. "Walk the plank!" he ordered.

The prisoners fell to their knees. "No, no, no," they cried.

"Fetch out the whip, Starkey," ordered Hook. "It's in the cabin."

"Aye, aye," said Starkey. And he strode into the cabin. Suddenly an awful screech wailed through the ship and died away. Then came an even more eerie, "Cock-a-doodle-doodle-do!"

"What was that?" shouted Hook, deadly pale. But no one could answer. And Starkey did not return from the cabin.

"All right, then," said the Captain. "We'll send those boys in to fight the doodle-doo. If they kill him, we're so much the better. If he kills them, we're none the worse."

Hastily the pirates pushed the boys into the dark cabin and shut the door. In a few minutes Peter untied them and gave them the weapons he had brought with him.

Outside the pirates were shivering in their boots, wondering if the doodle-doo was still alive. The cabin door opened. And now they heard a human cry. "Down boys, and at them!" Peter's voice rang out. In another moment the clash of arms resounded throughout the ship. One by one the pirates were either done away with or escaped. Finally, the only one who remained was Hook himself. He held off everyone by lashing out with his sinister hook.

Suddenly Peter leaped in front of him, sword in hand. The two enemies looked at one another for a long moment. Then their swords crossed. Hook slashed at Peter with his sword and clawed the air with his hook, but Peter flitted out of the way of every thrust and drove the pirate back steadily. Hook saw his last chance — to jump into the sea and swim for shore. He turned and dove. But there was no escape. Down below, just as he dove, he saw the crocodile — waiting for him.

Now Peter freed Wendy from the mast. She dressed everyone's wounds with bandages and put them all to bed in the pirates' bunks. Peter strutted proudly on deck until at last he fell asleep beside Long Tom, the big gun that would shoot no more.

In the morning they were all up early, wearing the clothes the pirates had left behind them. The boys tumbled out on deck with a true sailor's roll. Peter decided to pilot them part of the way home. And so they sailed away—with him at the wheel as Captain and Wendy in the galley as cook.

HOME AGAIN

Between sailing and flying the children arrived back at the little house they had left so long ago. Sure enough, in spite of their fears, the window was open. Leaving Peter and the Lost Boys outside, Wendy, John and Michael flew in to see if anyone was waiting for them.

They looked around the bedroom. By the light of the fire they saw Nana's old kennel. Instead of Nana, a man was curled up, asleep, inside.

"Goodness!" said Wendy, going up close. "There's a man in the kennel."

"It's Father!" exclaimed John.

Sure enough, it was Mr. Darling, who had been so ashamed of putting Nana out on the night the children had gone away that he had vowed to live in the kennel until they returned.

"Let me see Father," said Michael, who had almost forgotten what he looked like. "Well, he is not as big as the pirate I killed," he grumbled—but his disappointment did not last long.

Just then Mrs. Darling came into the room. She could hardly believe her eyes to find all her children home again. She woke her husband and called in Nana, and everyone was very happy.

It almost seemed as though Neverland had been a dream, except that the Lost Boys were waiting outside. Wendy called them in and asked her mother if she wouldn't adopt them. Mrs. Darling said, "Of course." And Mr. Darling took them all off with him to find places to sleep.

Peter had been hovering outside the window in the starry night. Now he came in. "Good-by, Wendy," he said sadly.

"Oh, dear, are you really going away?"

"Yes," he said, "I am going back to Neverland."

"You will be lonely," she said. "Who will tell you stories and take care of you?"

"You could, if you came back with me," he said temptingly.

"No," she said, "I am home now and mustn't leave. But every year at spring-cleaning time, if you will call for me, I will come and stay with you for a week."

Peter agreed quickly. He had so little idea of time that a year was like a day, and a day like a year. And so, crowing happily at Wendy's promise, he flew away into the night and back to Neverland.